This book is dedicated to my husband Brian, for his endless support of me and my dreams and for being the best dog daddy to Samson ever!

www.mascotbooks.com

Samson's Tail

For more information, please contact:
Mascot Books
620 Herndon Parkway, Suite 320
Herndon, VA 20170
info@mascotbooks.com

Library of Congress Control Number: 2019908481

CPSIA Code: PRT0819A
ISBN-13: 978-1-64307-483-2

Printed in the United States

As the van pulled up to a concrete building with a big, metal gate, Samson's tummy dropped. Would this be better than the shelter, or worse? The building had tall fences, and a sign that read *Birchwood Prison*. The gate swung open and the van pulled in. Samson was now a prison dog.

The inmate who he would be living with for the next month and a half was named Trevor. When Samson first saw the mountain of a man that Trevor was, he shrank and pinned his tail down between his legs.

Trevor had dark hair and tattoos covering both of his arms. His eyes were sad and his forehead showed lines from stress and worry. Trevor had not smiled since he entered the prison almost five months ago. His voice was strong but gentle as he offered his hand for Samson to sniff.

During their first few days together, Trevor and Samson spent most of their free time in their cell. They both preferred to stay to themselves, withdrawn from the daily prison routines. They soon grew to appreciate that they were no longer alone.

One night, it was especially loud. All the banging and yelling made Samson shake. Trevor reached down and scooped Samson up in his arms. Samson finally felt safe.

Sometimes when they were alone, Trevor spoke about his life before prison. They both had spent time out on the streets alone, and now they just wanted to find love. Trevor wanted something to be passionate and excited about, and Samson wanted the love of a forever family.

The prison guard yelled, "Lights out!" Trevor rubbed Samson's soft ears and smiled for the first time in a very long time.

Part of being a prison dog meant weekly training sessions with Trevor and all the other dogs and inmates. The dogs learned sit, stay, down, heel, off, and leave it to prepare them for adoption. At first, Samson would feel sick as they walked out to the yard. The strange dogs and new people made him tremble, his tail between his legs.

Samson struggled to understand what Trevor wanted. His worries made him breathe quickly, his tongue hanging out, wide-eyed. "It's okay, Samson, you're fine," Trevor said, trying to soothe Samson's nerves.

But, after about a week of training, Samson started to feel more comfortable and sat down on command.

Trevor looked excited, gave him a treat, and said, "Good boy!" Samson felt proud for the first time. From then on, whenever Trevor said, "Yes!" and gave him more treats, Samson's ears stood up and his tail gave a little wag.

Samson and Trevor were becoming best friends. They were both learning a lot and even became the stars of the prison program. Trevor was smiling, making friends, and even helping other inmates with their dog training. And Samson's tail was wagging all the time!

One night as they were just about to fall asleep, Trevor whispered, "Samson, thanks to you I finally found what I love. I'm gonna be a dog trainer when I get outta here next month!"

One cool, rainy day, Samson was taken out of his cell without Trevor. Before he left, he looked up at his friend one last time. Trevor knelt down and Samson raised his paw to shake, one of the many tricks Trevor had taught him. "You're ready, little buddy. Good luck!" Trevor said, beaming.

Samson looked over his shoulder as he pranced out the door. A happy couple stood outside. They had big smiles and friendly voices. Samson perked his ears and wagged his tail. Trevor had given him confidence. He was ready for the love of a forever family.

"I love him!" the woman said.

"He'll be the perfect addition to our family!" the man answered. Samson wagged his tail like crazy as they put him in the back of their car.

It was a long drive and Samson fell asleep a couple of times. He dreamed of his new life, and of Trevor, and smiled because he knew that they had both found the love that they always wanted.

THE
END

Author's Note

My husband and I adopted Samson from the DAWGS Prison Program owned by Steve and Amy Eckert in Pottsville, Pennsylvania, on April 18, 2015. This program saves dogs from shelters and places them in prisons. The dogs are trained all basic commands and live in a cell with their handler. Once the dogs have graduated from the program, they are placed in their forever homes.

The Massachusetts Department of Corrections found that having a canine program in a medium security prison decreased depression and aggression and increased morale among offenders and staff. According to the ASPCA website, 3.3 million dogs enter shelters each year in the United States and only 1.6 million of those dogs are adopted. If you can adopt from a prison program in your area, know that you are not only helping a dog, you are helping a human, too.

ABOUT THE AUTHOR

Mercy Hansen Mize has taught elementary school for sixteen years and has been an animal lover her entire life. In April of 2015, Mercy and her husband Brian adopted Samson from the DAWGS Prison Program and there began her passion for dog adoption and training. Since then, she and her husband have supported this amazing nonprofit organization which helps dogs, offenders, and forever families. *Samson's Tail* was inspired by this program and Mercy's desire to promote and educate others about its worthy cause. Therefore, a portion of the proceeds from the sales of *Samson's Tail* will go to support the DAWGS Prison Program.

ABOUT SAMSON

As a puppy, Samson was rescued from a shelter in North Carolina by Steve and Amy Eckert and placed in their DAWGS Prison Program in Pottsville, Pennsylvania. He started the program a shy, timid puppy and blossomed into a confident, happy dog. When he was approximately eight months of age, Samson was adopted into his forever family and now lives an exciting life! He practices agility, goes camping, plays on the beach, enjoys long hikes, regularly visits the local farmers' markets, loves to perform many tricks for his family and friends, and has lots of four-legged friends including dogs, cats, and horses! In addition to all of this fun, Samson has worked hard to earn his Canine Good Citizen certification and his Therapy Dog certification, which he uses to visit nursing homes and libraries regularly. Today, Samson is a very lucky and happy little dog whose tail rarely stops wagging!